THE BOOK OF
≡ ELEMENTAL ≡
POWERS

THE OFFICIAL GUIDE
TO THE WORLD OF NINJAGO!

Illustrated by AMEET Studio

Random House  New York

EDITOR'S NOTE

I've always dreamed about becoming a ninja someday. Delivering newspapers on the streets of Ninjago City, I've seen their battles up close. I've witnessed them using their elemental powers of fire, lightning, ice, earth, energy, and water.

I've seen villains using elemental powers, too. I'll never forget when I was in the middle of a fierce battle between the ninja and huge fire snakes! And more than once, Lord Garmadon's elemental power of Destruction almost destroyed the city I love for good.

Eventually, I started writing down what I knew about the ninja and the elemental powers. I researched elemental powers and how they work. How many powers are there? What's the strongest elemental power? Who are the Elemental Masters? I started out asking these simple questions, and what I learned led me into a world of adventure!

There is still so much we don't know about elemental powers. But I hope you'll like reading about what I've found so far.

Ninjago forever!

J.

CONTENTS

WHAT IS AN ELEMENTAL POWER?

"Elemental power comes from within, like courage."
—Sorla of the Great Lake

In the realm of Ninjago, elements are the prime forces that make up the world: Fire, Ice, Earth, Lightning, and more.

We do the best we can to use and benefit from elements. We use fire to cook and stay warm. We use ice to preserve our food.

But a small group of beings have the ability to do more than use the elements—they master and control them. They are Elemental Masters, and their power over the elements comes from deep within. But how did that power get there?

WHERE IT ALL BEGAN

The original Elemental Masters can be traced back to the First Spinjitzu Master, the creator of the realm of Ninjago. They were skilled fighters and the First Spinjitzu Master's guardians. He granted them their own special elemental powers, to help him protect the realm. Together, they formed the Elemental Alliance. When the Elemental Masters combine their powers, almost no force of evil can stop them.

WHAT MAKES AN ELEMENTAL MASTER?

"Each Elemental Master is endowed with an elemental power that has been passed down through generations." —Garmadon

If your mother or father was an Elemental Master, chances are you will be, too, and you'll have the same power your parent had. For example, Kai the Fire Ninja got his powers from his father, and his sister, Nya, got her powers from her mother, a Water Ninja.

An Elemental Master is not born being able to use their power. It must be awakened in them. And the more a Master works with their power, the more they can achieve. Masters who overcome fear and doubt can manifest an elemental dragon.

An Elemental Master has the ability to unlock their True Potential—the first step to mastering a higher level of Spinjitzu. When this happens, the Master's body and their element become one, and the Master's powers expand.

However, being an Elemental Master doesn't automatically mean you will use your great powers for good. While some have used their powers to protect Ninjago world, others have used them to cause chaos and destruction.

DID YOU KNOW?

An Elemental Master can pass on their power to someone who is not their child. When the Master of Ice visited the young Nindroid named Zane, he was so impressed by the boy that he bestowed his powers on him.

FIRE

"If you give me food, I will grow. If you give me a drink, I will die."
—Ninjigma riddle about Fire

Fire is one of the elements of creation and one of the four main elemental powers. Some claim that with its orange and red Spinjitzu tornado, it is the most spectacular of all the elements.

FIRE POWER

The element of fire can grant the power of Pyrokinesis, allowing the user to shoot fireballs and melt matter. Extremely effective for fighting all kinds of villains, these awesome abilities can also be quite handy at home for:

organizing garden parties

lighting dark spaces

fixing metal items

DID YOU KNOW?

Masters of Fire can also manipulate their element from existing sources. The mastery of fire often comes hand in hand with unique artistic talents.

THE FIRE NINJA

Ninjago realm's Master of Fire is Kai. Making a living as a simple blacksmith, Kai had no idea of his incredible hidden potential until he met Master Wu. Kai's bravery, impulsive personality, and fierce temper mirror the fire within him. His strong sense of justice makes him stubborn, and he'll stop at nothing if he has put his mind to it!

Could Kai be any more awesome?

ELEMENTAL FAMILY

Nya

Kai's younger sister. He's often overprotective of her, although she has proven many times that she can take care of herself. After all, Nya is also a trained ninja and the Elemental Master of Water.

Ray

Kai got his elemental power from his father, who, in his young days, was Wu's best friend. Together they had many adventures before Ray settled down and had a family.

Maya

Long before Kai and Nya were born, Kai's mother, the Elemental Master of Water, had fought alongside her husband and other Elemental Masters in the Serpentine Wars.

THE POWERS OF THE ELEMENTAL MASTER OF FIRE

As the Master of Fire, Kai is capable of wielding the Sword of Fire—one of the legendary Golden Weapons forged and used by the First Master of Spinjitzu to create the realm of Ninjago.

Only Kai could make a bond with the powerful Fire Dragon, the guardian of the Sword of Fire. Kai called him Flame, and he was the first ninja from Wu's team to tame his dragon.

It took a lot of training for Kai to fully utilize the powers of the Sword of Fire. By focusing his mind on his weapon, Kai learned how to summon an elemental vehicle—the awesome fiery Blade Cycle.

CREATURES OF FIRE

There are certain Serpentine who have Fire powers—the Pyro Vipers. Many years ago, they were merely Hypnobrai, pyramid builders serving King Mambo V. In modern times, they were resurrected by Aspheera, a Serpentine sorceress, who infused them with the Fire power she had stolen from Kai.

FIRE PROTECTING THE NINJAGO WORLD

Over many years, Kai risked his life fighting alongside his ninja friends to protect the world of Ninjago against many dreadful villains. Here are just a few examples from a long list of the Fire Ninja's acts of courage and devotion.

Kai kept the Sword of Fire from falling into the hands of evil Lord Garmadon and the Skulkin warriors, thus keeping the world of Ninjago safe.

The Fire Ninja discovered that his destiny was to protect Lloyd Garmadon, the prophesied Green Ninja. That revelation enabled Kai to unlock his true potential, and also helped Lloyd in his struggle against the powerful Overlord.

When you take great risks, you sometimes suffer great defeat. When the ninja accidentally released the Serpentine sorceress, Aspheera, on Ninjago world, Kai launched a fire blast at her. She absorbed it with her staff, draining him of his elemental powers.

The Never-Realm was a frozen world kept alive by a sacred Hearth Fire. Kai had no powers when he encountered the dying Hearth Fire. But he found the power deep inside himself to keep the fire going.

In what might be his greatest battle ever, Kai battled the Forbidden Ice Dragon, Boreal, in the Never-Realm. Kai called on his True Potential to launch a fiery inferno at the beast, melting him.

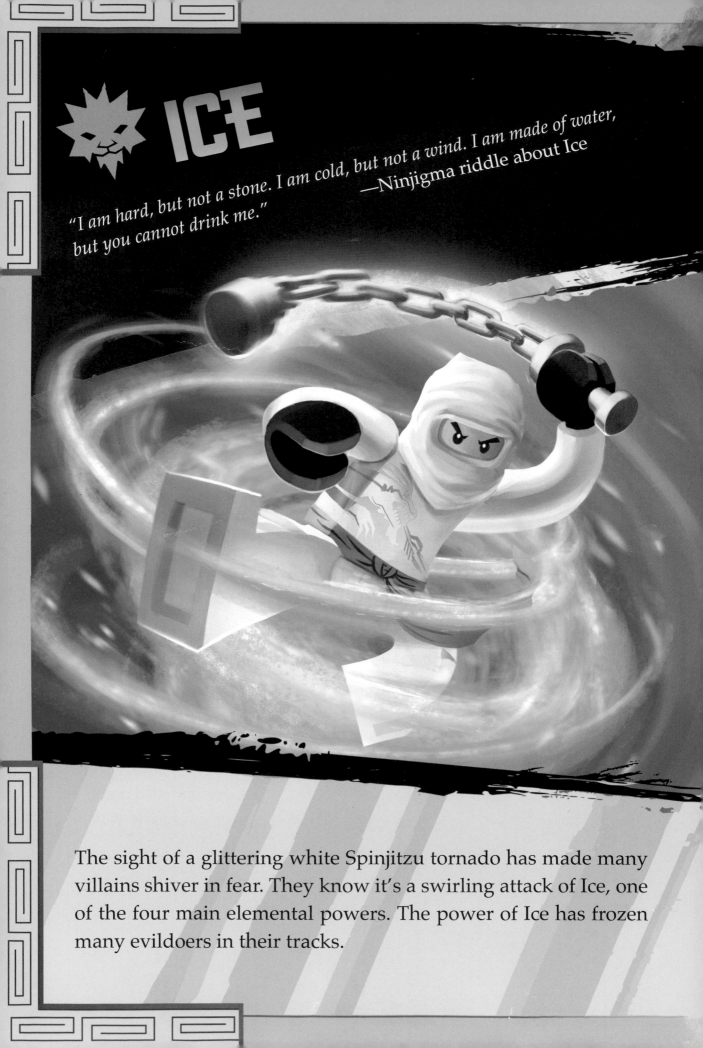

ICE

"I am hard, but not a stone. I am cold, but not a wind. I am made of water, but you cannot drink me."

—Ninjigma riddle about Ice

The sight of a glittering white Spinjitzu tornado has made many villains shiver in fear. They know it's a swirling attack of Ice, one of the four main elemental powers. The power of Ice has frozen many evildoers in their tracks.

ICE POWER

The element of Ice can be used to freeze outlaws—or make a delicious batch of cookie dough ice cream! Here are some other ways to use this frosty power:

instantly cool down hot drinks

ice surf

make ice shields and ice obstacles

DID YOU KNOW?

Master Wu recruited Zane when the boy was meditating at the bottom of a freezing pond. Zane could do it because he is a Nindroid.

THE ICE NINJA

He's known today as the Titanium Ninja, but Zane is still the Elemental Master of Ice. Zane is a Nindroid, built to protect those who cannot protect themselves. He has a "big heart," even though it's pure metal, and he is one of the most generous ninja when it comes to protecting Ninjago world.

Zane became known as the Titanium Ninja after building himself a new body out of the superstrong metal.

ELEMENTAL FAMILY

Dr. Julien

This inventor created Zane and raised him like a son. He gave Zane superior intelligence and physical skills, but not his ice powers.

The Past Elemental Master of Ice

This white-haired warrior fought with the other Elemental Masters during the Serpentine Wars. He had no children, so at the end of his life, he passed his powers on to Zane—who had no idea about the gift he'd been given.

THE POWERS OF THE ELEMENTAL MASTER OF ICE

Only the Master of Ice can wield the Shurikens of Ice. These icy throwing stars fly through the air with the biting power of a snowstorm, and will always return to Zane's hands after he throws them.

Talk about fresh breath! Shard, the guardian dragon of the Shurikens of Ice, breathes pure ice. Zane called on his logical skills to convince Shard to ride with him.

Zane was afraid to accept his new form as the Titanium Ninja. Once he conquered that fear, he unlocked his ability to summon the Titanium Dragon.

When Aspheera banished Zane to the Never-Realm, he lost his memory and was tricked into becoming the evil Ice Emperor. Then he used his Ice Scepter, powered by the Scroll of Forbidden Spinjitzu, to create the Blizzard Warriors and plunge the Never-Realm into eternal winter.

CREATURE OF ICE

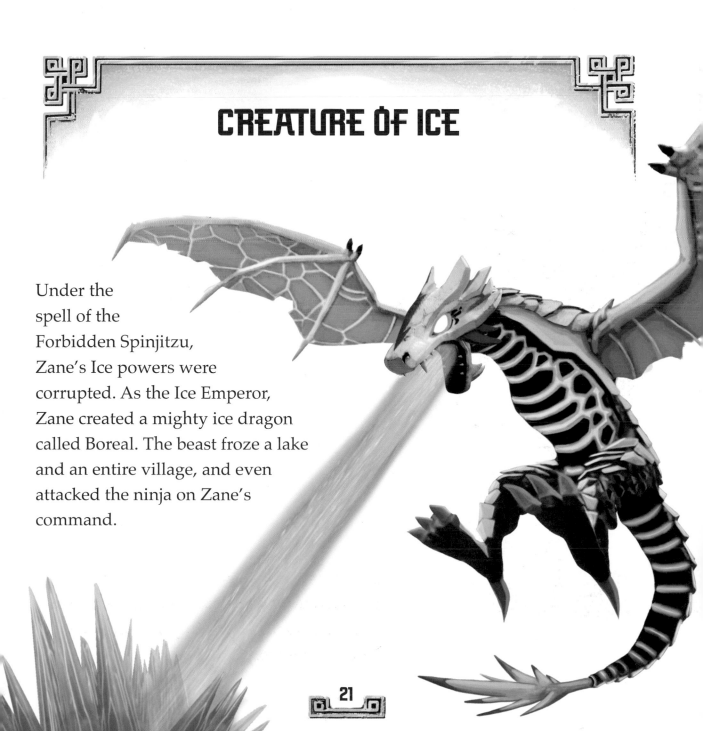

Under the spell of the Forbidden Spinjitzu, Zane's Ice powers were corrupted. As the Ice Emperor, Zane created a mighty ice dragon called Boreal. The beast froze a lake and an entire village, and even attacked the ninja on Zane's command.

ICE POWERS PROTECTING NINJAGO

"There is nothing that will hold me back. I know who I am," Zane said, when he discovered he was a robot. Then he unleashed his ice power just in time to save the ninja from the dangerous Treehorn creatures and their creepy queen. He was the first ninja to unlock his True Potential.

When the Overlord attacked the people of Ninjago City, the ninja couldn't stop him. Zane unleashed a massive frozen blast at the powerful villain, sacrificing his Nindroid body to save the city.

Zane battled Mr. E, a Nindroid member of the Sons of Garmadon biker gang, in the middle of a hot desert. Zane fought through the heat and pummeled the metal miscreant with several ice punches.

When the ninja battled Aspheera, Zane trapped her inside a block of ice. He saved his friends, but his action got him sent to the Never-Realm by the Serpentine sorceress.

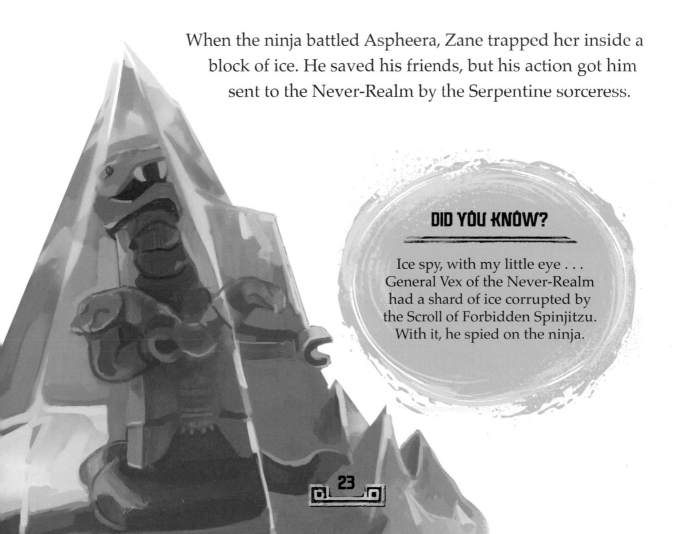

DID YOU KNOW?

Ice spy, with my little eye . . . General Vex of the Never-Realm had a shard of ice corrupted by the Scroll of Forbidden Spinjitzu. With it, he spied on the ninja.

EARTH

"I am under your feet, but also touch the sky. When I move, buildings fall."
—Ninjigma riddle about Earth

The immensely strong power of Earth is always astounding to witness, especially when it's a Spinitzu tornado filled with whirling rocks. That is why it takes its place as one of the four main elemental powers.

EARTH POWER

Those who connect to the element of Earth can manipulate rocks, dirt, and sand. That power manifests in different ways:

while making a sandcastle

as superhuman strength

in an Earth elemental shield

DID YOU KNOW?

The symbol of Earth resembles a gorilla—an animal known for its strength.

THE EARTH NINJA

Before he met Master Wu, Cole was a restless young man, exploring Ninjago Island in search of new challenges. Then he joined the ninja team and found his purpose. Cole is as strong as a mountain and as steady as a boulder, but his heart is as soft as the cupcakes he craves.

The ninja love to tease Cole about his love of food, but his dancing skills are earth-shattering.

ELEMENTAL FAMILY

Lilly

Cole's mother passed her powers on to Cole when she gave birth to him. Years before, she'd bravely battled a dragon known as the Grief-Bringer to save the people of the Kingdom of Shintaro.

Lou

Cole's dad is a singing, dancing performer who wanted his son to follow in his footsteps. But he's proud that Cole became a ninja.

Elemental Master of Earth

Cole's grandfather fought with the Elemental Masters against the Serpentine.

Krag

Cole thought this Yeti in the Never-Realm was a threat at first. But when Cole realized that Krag was the last of his kind, the two became good friends.

THE POWERS OF THE ELEMENTAL MASTER OF EARTH

Cole wielded the Scythe of Quakes, one of the Four Golden Weapons used by the First Spinjitzu Master to create the realm of Ninjago. It can cut through solid stone and cause the ground to shake and crack.

Cole had to overcome his fear of dragons so he could bond with the Earth Dragon who guarded the Scythe of Quakes. He named him Rocky.

When Cole taps into his True Potential, he becomes practically indestructible and his superstrength reaches mountainous heights.

Bam! Cole became the first Master of Earth to use the Earth Punch. He channels the power of magma through his arms to deliver a battle-ending blow.

Cole once piloted the Earth Driller, a vehicle that could travel over rough terrain as well as power through the underground. It was also handy for avoiding traffic.

CREATURE OF EARTH

Slab is a mighty dragon with the powers of Earth. He was captured by the Dragon Hunters in the Realm of Oni and Dragon, and forced to battle their enemies. Slab can bury opponents by blasting sand from his mouth. The ninja freed Slab, and Cole later bonded with him to help save the citizens of Ninjago City.

EARTH POWERS PROTECTING NINJAGO

When Cole saved a baby from the Sons of Garmadon, he thought he was doing a good deed. Then Cole discovered the child was Master Wu, who had reverted to an infant after touching a Time Reversal Blade. Cole's kind heart had saved Master Wu—and the future of Ninjago!

Cole's greatest challenge came when he accidentally became a ghost. With his close connection to Earth broken, Cole thought he couldn't be a ninja. But he embraced his ghostly powers before he became human again, proving that he has a rock-steady spirit.

When the ninja were trapped inside a museum with the Pyro Vipers, Cole helped take them down with his powerful Earth Punch.

Cole performed a Spinjitzu Burst to save the Kingdom of Shintaro. Any ninja has the potential to perform the move if they are surrounded by their element, but for ages, only Earth Masters knew how to do it.

DID YOU KNOW?

Before Cole knew that the baby he'd saved was Wu, he named him "Cole Jr."

LIGHTNING

"I light up the sky, but I am not the sun. My kiss is deadly, but I am not a snake."
—Ninjigma riddle about Lightning

It's no shock that Lightning is one of the four main elemental powers. Lightning is pure electricity—and electricity powers the realm of Ninjago. Jay always gets a charge from creating a Lightning Spinjitzu tornado that crackles with energy!

LIGHTNING POWER

The Master of Lightning can control, absorb, and redirect electricity. With practice, a Master can learn to:

overload electronic devices

create a defensive electrical force field

shoot lightning bolts

shock opponents

THE LIGHTNING NINJA

Jay is the Master of Lightning in the realm of Ninjago. Give him a problem and he'll brainstorm an invention to solve it. He brightens up every situation with his good nature and corny jokes. These things combined with his lightning-fast fighting skills make him a great ninja.

Jay always brings an extra spark of energy to the ninja team.

ELEMENTAL FAMILY

Edna and Ed Walker

Jay's parents adopted him when he was a baby. They encouraged Jay to tinker with all of the motors and metal in the junkyard they owned.

The Past Elemental Master of Lightning

Jay doesn't know much about his mom, except that back in the day, she fought alongside the Elemental Masters in the Serpentine Wars.

Cliff Gordon

Imagine discovering that your father is actually your favorite actor! That happened to Jay, who is a huge fan of Fritz Donnegan, an adventurous character played by his birth dad.

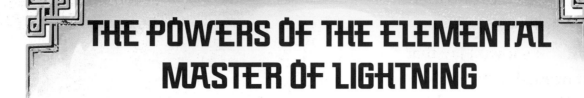

Wielding the Nunchucks of Lightning is like harnessing the power of a storm—they're pure energy, and thunder booms when they are used. It takes a skilled Master to control them.

Some say that in an attempt to tame the Lightning Dragon, Jay used the power of a good joke. But the dragon didn't have a sense of humor. So Jay invented a device to make the dragon's roar louder, and that did the trick. Jay named the dragon Wisp.

Lightning belongs in the sky—and Jay has piloted a few flying vehicles. His first was the Storm Fighter, a speedy jet sparking with electric energy.

Jay sometimes jokes that his first kiss with Nya was "electric." It showed Jay that he just needed to be himself, and it allowed him to achieve his True Potential. In this form, Jay can use the power of electricity to fly and travel through electric currents.

CREATURE OF LIGHTNING

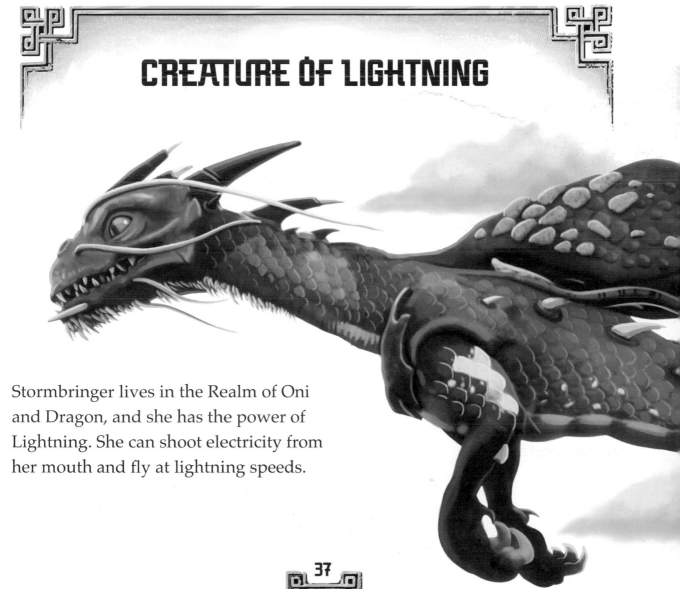

Stormbringer lives in the Realm of Oni and Dragon, and she has the power of Lightning. She can shoot electricity from her mouth and fly at lightning speeds.

LIGHTNING PROTECTING NINJAGO

Jay broke his leg in a brutal island competition in Master Chen's Tournament of Elements. But that didn't stop him— he found the ElectroMech and used it to battle Master Chen's evil henchman, Clouse.

Things seemed hopeless when Vermillion warriors kidnapped Jay's mom, Edna, from the junkyard. Jay's dad, Ed, gave him a motorcycle with massive wheels he'd built, called Desert Lightning. Jay supercharged it with electricity and zoomed away to rescue his mom.

One of Jay's biggest battles took place against an AI villain named Unagami, who attacked Ninjago in the form of the Empire Dragon. Jay helped calm down Unagami by revealing what they had in common—they'd both been abandoned by their parents.

When evil Prince Kalmaar attacked the *Hydro Bounty*, an underwater sub, the ninja team was almost sank. But Jay risked his life to recharge the batteries.

THE YIN-YANG PROMISE

Water and electricity shouldn't mix, right? But Jay and Nya turned a strong friendship into an even stronger love for each other. Jay was thrilled when Nya pledged to be the Yang to his Yin.

WATER

"While the Earth is strong and air is fluid, water can be both strong and fluid."
—Master Wu

Water has the power to make things grow, put out fires, and cool us down—but as a tidal wave, it has the incredible power of destruction, too. Many villains have fled at the sight of Nya's Spinjitzu tornado of water.

WATER POWER

Water is the only elemental power that can stop ghosts! The Master of Water can also manipulate water to do some amazing things, both in battle and in everyday life. The Master of Water can:

make it rain

make a water shield

make a water blast

DID YOU KNOW?

Ice is frozen water, and a skilled Master of Water can manipulate ice—although not at the same level as a Master of Ice.

THE WATER NINJA

"I've discovered Nya's weakness—feeling weak," Master Wu said while Nya was training to be Master of Water. She gave up too easily when put in a position to fail. Once Nya realized it was okay to fail sometimes, she unleashed a dam of incredible powers.

Nya donned the Samurai X suit before she became the Water Ninja.

ELEMENTAL FAMILY

Kai

Fire and Water are opposite elements, but Nya and her brother actually have a lot in common. They both have strong personalities and a hunger to fight evil.

Maya

Nya inherited her Water powers from her mother, Maya. The two of them bonded when they worked together to battle Prince Kalmaar of the underwater kingdom of Merlopia.

Ray

Nya's father is the former Master of Fire. The villain Krux captured Ray and Maya and forced them to build him weapons and vehicles. The family was reunited when Krux was defeated.

THE POWERS OF THE ELEMENTAL MASTER OF WATER

Nya blocked an attack of ghostly arrows shot at *Destiny's Bounty* by summoning a tall wave of ocean water. Then she waved bye-bye to the ghosts!

Nya discovered her True Potential just in time to save Ninjago world from a true terror—the Preeminent, the monstrous, tentacled ruler of the Cursed Realm. In a spectacular show of power, Nya defeated the Preeminent and destroyed the entire Cursed Realm in a massive tidal wave.

While trying to stop Prince Kalmaar from awakening a legendary sea serpent, Nya discovered that she had the power to communicate with whales—a power she shared with the First Elemental Master of Water.

THE LEGEND OF NYAD

The first Elemental Master of Water—and Nya's ancestor—was a brave Merlopian warrior named Nyad. She fought her greatest battle deep in the Endless Sea against an enormous sea serpent called Wojira. Legend says that long ago, the monster was awakened and Nyad defeated her on the last day of the Battle of Nine Days. To do so, Nyad had to lose herself in her elemental power and become one with the sea. She was never seen again.

ENERGY

"It's some kind of energy, or green light! Like all our Elemental Powers rolled into one!"
—Cole

It is believed that Energy, also known as Green Power, is a combination of the four main elemental powers: Fire, Lightning, Ice, and Earth. The power uses the strength of these elements to create powerful energy attacks.

ENERGY POWER

Energy is what propels the world forward—we use it for light and heat, and to go far and fast. Energy can create life and also destroy it. The master who controls this power can tap into the energy of the elements and harness it to:

create energy blasts, balls, and beams	construct a strong energy shield	propel forward quickly

THE PROPHECY

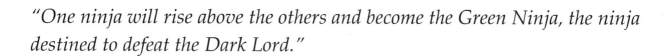

"One ninja will rise above the others and become the Green Ninja, the ninja destined to defeat the Dark Lord."

When Kai, Cole, Jay and Zane were a newly formed ninja team, they discovered a scroll with this ancient prophecy written on it. They each dreamed of becoming the Green Ninja—and were shocked to learn that the destined one was Lloyd, son of the evil Lord Garmadon!

THE GREEN NINJA

Lloyd Garmadon's journey is one of a true hero. He started out as a troublemaking boy who wanted to be just like his evil dad, and ended up as the leader of the ninja team. While he wields great power, Lloyd is known for being calm and level-headed.

Lloyd is the youngest ninja, but some say he is the wisest.

THE POWERS
OF THE GREEN NINJA

Lloyd learned to summon an Elemental Energy Dragon after he learned to face his fears.

"A ninja never quits!" Lloyd cried when he accepted his destiny as the Ultimate Spinjitzu Master. He unlocked his True Potential and became the Golden Ninja.

Lloyd can use his energy to power vehicles—like the Titan Mech, a large robot with a human pilot. It was destroyed during a battle with the Forbidden Ice Dragon, Boreal.

DID YOU KNOW?

Lloyd tried hard to be evil when he was a kid, but his evil deeds were mostly pranks— like dyeing Zane's ninja suit pink and scaring Cole with rubber snakes.

GOLDEN POWER

"The Golden Power needs to be protected, honored. Evil forces will seek it, try to take it for their own."
—Garmadon

Instead of asking what the Golden Power can do, it's better to ask—what can't Golden Power do? Golden Power can create and destroy. It is truly the ultimate elemental power.

THE GOLDEN NINJA

A Golden Ninja needs a golden ride, right? Lloyd used Golden Energy to create vehicles just by thinking about them—like his Golden Cycle.

ELEMENTAL FAMILY

Lord Garmadon

Lloyd has a roller-coaster relationship with his father. They've battled each other, but have had peaceful times learning from each other, too.

Master Wu

Lloyd's uncle trained him in the ninja arts.

Misako

Lloyd's mother helps the ninja team with her knowledge of Ninjago history, her good advice, and her Spinjitzu training. She once defeated a Vermillion with a cooking pan!

THE POWERS OF THE GOLDEN NINJA

Golden Power is theoretically infinite, but as the Golden Ninja, Lloyd has used that power in special ways.

Before he knew he would become the Golden Ninja, Lloyd found out he was able to power the First Spinjitzu Master's Golden Mech.

As the Golden Ninja, Lloyd could summon the beautiful Golden Dragon. It's too bad he still can't summon one. Showing up on a Golden Dragon is a sure way to impress a date!

When Lloyd was traveling with his father, he used his Golden Power to literally move a mountain and save Garmadon's life.

When the evil Overlord infected Nya and residents of Ninjago City with Dark Matter, Lloyd's Golden Power healed them.

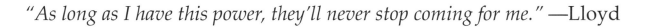

HOW LLOYD LOST HIS GOLDEN POWER

"As long as I have this power, they'll never stop coming for me." —Lloyd

Brave Lloyd may have defeated the Overlord, but the evil entity was not destroyed. He plotted to steal Lloyd's Golden Power. To save the world of Ninjago, Lloyd shared his Golden Power with Kai, Zane, Cole, and Jay.

THE ORIGIN OF THE GOLDEN POWER

As legend has it, Golden Power is the strongest elemental power. The first known being to wield it was the First Spinjitzu Master, the child of the Oni and Dragon.

THE FIRST SPINJITZU MASTER

What we currently know is that long, long ago, there was only one realm: the Realm of Oni and Dragon. Oni are creatures of Destruction, and Dragons are creatures of Creation. For centuries, the Oni and Dragon fought fiercely. Then a child was born of both worlds: a child of light and darkness, who had a special Golden Power.

This child grew up and tried to unite the realm, but when he saw there would never be peace, he left. He used his power to forge Four Golden Weapons. And he used those weapons to create the islands of Ninjago. It was there, in Ninjago world, that he also created the art of Spinjitzu. From then on, he became known as the First Spinjitzu Master.

CREATOR OF THE ELEMENTS

Master Wu always believed that his father was the creator of all the elements, but he recently learned the truth: before he was born, the powers of Water, Storm, and Wave ruled. And there is still much we don't know about the elemental powers.

POWERS OF THE FIRST SPINJITZU MASTER

While some believe there was no limit to his powers, the First Spinjitzu Master created several tools that he used with it.

The First Spinjitzu Master befriended the legendary mother of all dragons, Firstbourne. Together, they created the golden Dragon Armor, which allowed them to fly together.

Using metal from the Golden Peaks, the First Spinjitzu Master forged the Four Golden Weapons of Spinjitzu: the Sword of Fire, the Nunchucks of Lightning, the Scythe of Quakes, and the Shurikens of Ice.

When combined with the power of Creation, the Four Golden Weapons can become a Mega Weapon. It can be used to create anything your heart desires—mega good, or mega bad!

HIS GREATEST OPPONENT

The Overlord emerged from the shadows to battle the First Spinjitzu Master. He lost, and the First Spinjitzu Master banished him to the Dark Island. There, existing as a spirit, the incredibly powerful Overlord plotted to return and get his revenge.

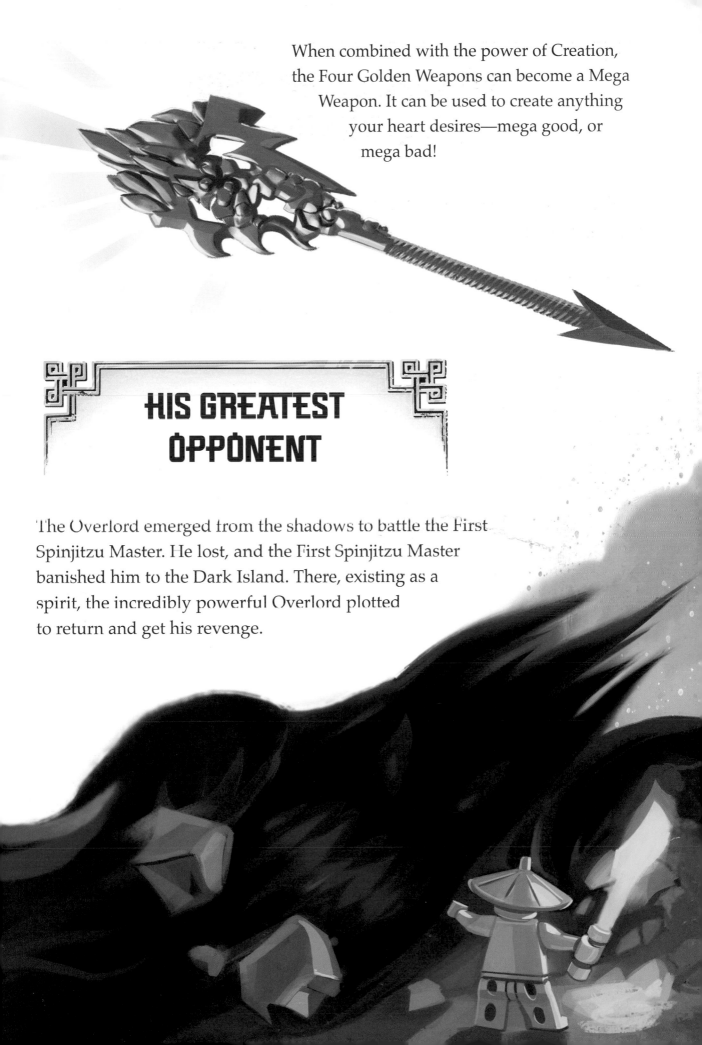

THE LEGEND OF THE GOLDEN MASTER

For centuries, the Serpentine shared this legend with their children: *"Since the first dawn, the elders have spoken of the Curse of the Golden Master, when he who had the powers equal to the First Spinjitzu Master would rise and usher in the last of the setting suns. With no equal adversary, his power will go unmatched. His destructive rule will change the shape of the world. And he will not stop until every man, woman, and Serpentine are enslaved under his control."*

THE OVERLORD BECOMES THE GOLDEN MASTER

The Overlord stole some of Lloyd's Golden Power and recovered the remains of the Four Golden Weapons. He reforged them to make the Golden Armor—also known as the Armor of the Golden Master—and unleashed an attack on New Ninjago City.

THE END OF THE GOLDEN MASTER

Zane sacrificed himself by discharging all of his power on the Golden Master, destroying the Overlord. But Ninjago needs both Darkness and Light to remain in perfect balance. Does this mean the Overlord might return some day?

DARKNESS

"In order for there to be light, there must be shadow. And within shadow, there is darkness, the blackest of darkness that existed from the very beginning."
—Misako

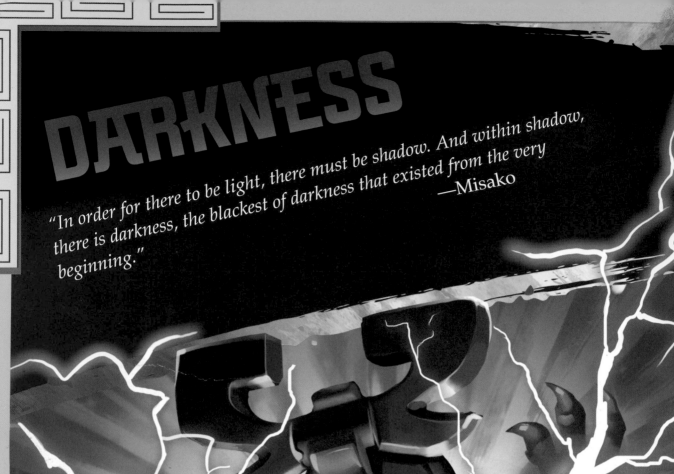

Spinjitzu represents all that is Light, and the Overlord represents the Darkness. But the Overlord never wanted balance—he wanted Darkness to rule.

POWERS OF THE OVERLORD

The Overlord used his mastery of Darkness to battle the First Spinjitzu Master long ago, and more recently, the ninja. With Darkness, he was able to:

plunge Ninjago world into gloom

corrupt the souls of others with Dark Matter

shoot beams that destroy anything they touch

FORMS OF DARKNESS

The Overlord has manifested as several different Dark forms—each one uniquely terrifying in its own way.

Darkness Emerges

Darkness first crept out of the shadows to challenge the First Spinjitzu Master as a large, shadowy shape.

Lord Garmadon Possessed

The Overlord used Lord Garmadon as a pawn to battle Ninjago world, and then took over his body.

Dragon of Darkness

Possessing Lord Garmadon's body allowed the Overlord to transform into an enormous black dragon with glowing purple eyes.

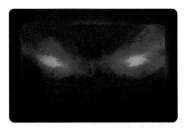

The Digital Overlord

Lloyd destroyed the dragon, but the Overlord's spirit survived and infected the Ninjago City computer network.

SERVANTS OF THE OVERLORD

The Overlord may be hugely powerful, but his plans would never have succeeded without the help of his minions.

The Stone Army

These indestructible warriors were created by the Overlord using a mysterious stone-like material. These soldiers weren't the sharpest rocks in the pile, though. You might call them blockheads!

Nindroids

The Digital Overlord briefly took control over P.I.X.A.L., an android assistant to inventor Cyrus Borg. She created an army of robot ninja for him based on Zane's blueprints. Of course, none had the same skills or spirit as the one and only Master of Ice!

DID YOU KNOW?

Dareth, the self-named Brown Ninja, accidentally put on a helmet that allowed him to briefly command the Stone Army.

CREATION

"Creation, like Destruction, is not an element—it is an Elemental essence—an energy. When the energy of creation is used with the elements, the results can be amazing." —from a document found in the Ancient Library of Domu

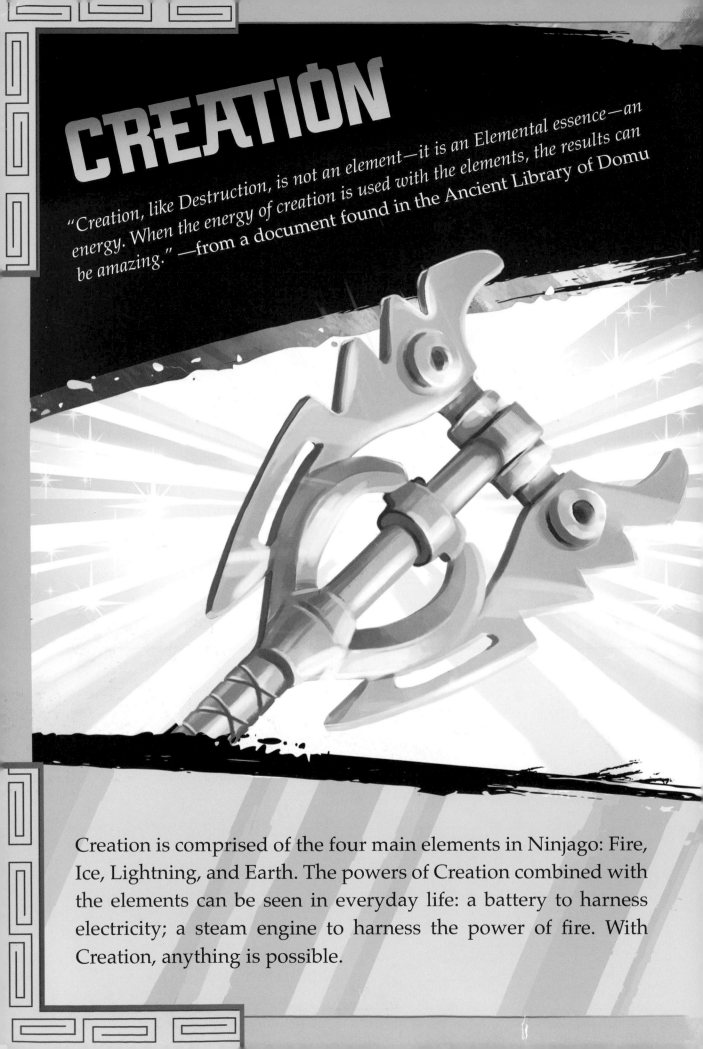

Creation is comprised of the four main elements in Ninjago: Fire, Ice, Lightning, and Earth. The powers of Creation combined with the elements can be seen in everyday life: a battery to harness electricity; a steam engine to harness the power of fire. With Creation, anything is possible.

As a child of the Dragons and Oni, the First Spinjitzu Master was born with both the energy of Creation and Destruction. He passed them on to his sons, Wu and Garmadon. The energy of Creation was dominant in Wu, and the energy of Destruction was dominant in Garmadon.

The two brothers represent balance. Without Creation, there is nothing to destroy. Without Destruction, there is no room to create. Maybe that is why it is impossible to imagine the world of Ninjago with just Wu or just Lord Garmadon.

POWERS OF CREATION

The First Spinjitzu Master used the Four Golden Weapons to create the Ninjago Islands. The ninja have used them as well.

With the Golden Weapons, the ninja can perform a move called the Tornado of Creation. This spinning tornado picks up objects in its path and creates new objects of them—like the Ultra Sonic Raider they used to defeat the Great Devourer . . .

or a ferris wheel that captured all the Skulkin warriors.

DID YOU KNOW?

Master Wu has warned the ninja that while the Tornado of Creation may be the most powerful move in Spinjitzu, it is also the most dangerous if it is not done right.

MASTER WU

He may look like a mild-mannered, tea-drinking old man, but Master Wu is a skilled ninja master with incredible powers. It is unknown if Wu has unlocked his True Potential yet—and if he does, if it will involve the energy of Creation.

When Master Wu balances his abilities, he creates a golden, spinning Spinjitzu tornado.

DID YOU KNOW?

Master Wu's pet is . . . a *chicken*? She's no ordinary chicken—she has Lightning powers, and Wu has used her to keep the ninja on their toes.

Like the other ninja, Master Wu can summon his own dragon. He rarely rides his dragon, but he relied on him when the battling the ghostly Morro—the Master of Wind.

WU'S GREATEST CREATION

"You four are the chosen ones who will protect the weapons of Spinjitzu from Lord Garmadon."
—Master Wu

Master Wu didn't need elemental powers to make his greatest creation—the ninja team!

To protect the Four Golden Weapons of Spinjitzu from his evil brother, Lord Garmadon, Wu tracked down and recruited four boys, descendants of Elemental Masters. Then he trained them in the art of Spinjitzu to guard the weapons.

WU'S GREATEST OPPONENT

Master Wu has guided the ninja to fight just about every villain that has attacked Ninjago world, from skeleton warriors to ancient demons. But his greatest opponent has always been his brother, Garmadon. The brothers have always been opposites—just as Creation is the opposite of Destruction. Together, they represent the balance of these two forces.

DESTRUCTION

"Do not confuse Destruction with Darkness. Darkness feeds on Creation. It needs life to make evil. Destruction fears Creation. Destruction only wants to erase all life."
—from a document found in the Ancient Library of Domu

Destruction can be scary, but it is also necessary. You have to cut down a tree to build a fire, or break through ice to catch a fish. Without destruction, there can be no new beginnings.

DEMONS OF DESTRUCTION

With their long horns, fiery eyes and razor-sharp claws, the demon-like Oni are shapeshifters with the ability to destroy. The race of Oni that once warred with the Dragons in the First Realm are known as the Bringers of Doom.

The Oni left three relics in Ninjago world: the Mask of Deception, the Mask of Vengeance, and the Mask of Hatred. Together, they can be used to open the portal to the Departed Realm and bring back one with Oni blood.

Known as the Omega, the leader of the Oni yearned to engulf the world of Ninjago in a cloud of Destruction. After thousands of years in retreat, the Omega led the Oni back to Ninjago, but the ninja ultimately stopped them with a Tornado of Creation.

LORD GARMADON

"I've played many roles. Worn many masks. Father. Husband. Brother. Teacher. But only one was summoned back—Destroyer!"

Lord Garmadon uttered these words to his son, Lloyd, after an evil princess named Harumi brought him back from the Departed Realm. In that form, Lord Garmadon reached his True Potential as an instrument of Destruction. But his path to becoming the Destroyer was a long and complicated one.

PATH TO DESTRUCTION

Son and Brother

Garmadon inherited the essence of Destruction from the Oni part of his father, the First Spinjitzu Master. He was a happy child until the day he was bitten by the Great Devourer. The venom worked slowly on Garmadon, gradually filling his veins with evil.

The First Lord Garmadon

After being banished to the Underworld by Wu, Lord Garmadon sprouted four arms so that he could wield the Golden Weapons by himself. Rumor has it that he became an excellent juggler, too.

Lloyd's Father

Purified of the Devourer's evil, Lord Garmadon became Master Garmadon. He promised to live a peaceful life and spend time with his son, Lloyd, until fate sent him to the Departed Realm.

Lord Garmadon Reborn

When Princess Harumi brought Lord Garmadon back from the Departed Realm, his Oni nature controlled him. He ruled Ninjago world as Emperor Garmadon.

Lord Garmadon the Oni

When the Omega tried to destroy the realm of Ninjago, Lord Garmadon transformed into his Oni form to level the playing field. Oni vs. Oni!

INSTRUMENTS OF DESTRUCTION

The Mega Weapon

Lord Garmadon used the Mega Weapon to create the ninja doppelgangers, evil versions of the ninja. They were easy to identify by their red, glowing eyes—and their less-than-impressive fighting skills.

The Garmatron

Lord Garmadon believed that the Overlord was building this doomsday machine just for him. The monster-sized tank launched Dark Matter missiles, which upset the balance between Light and Darkness in the realm. That meant the Overlord could return, so he possessed Garmadon's body, ruining all his fun.

The Colossus

When he ruled the world of Ninjago, Emperor Garmadon created an enormous stone giant, Colossus, to help him terrorize and control Ninjago City. At Emperor Garmadon's command, the huge creature destroyed everything in its path. In the end, this monster was really just a big pile of boulders.

DID YOU KNOW?

While he lived in the Underworld, Lord Garmadon dined on Condensed Evil—a black sludge filled with creepy crawlies. Did eating it make him even more evil? No one is sure. But he did claim that it was low in fat.

LORD GARMADON'S ARMIES OF DESTRUCTION

Why do evil masterminds have no problem getting followers? The more powerfully destructive Lord Garmadon became, the more dangerous his minions were.

The Skulkin

The Skulkin are bad to the bone, but they were not the most organized fighting force. Lord Garmadon thought they were a bunch of numbskulls. Even so, they gave Wu's newly formed ninja team a tough time.

The Stone Army

The Overlord created the Stone Army from an indestructible material from the Island of Darkness. Years later, he gave Lord Garmadon the Helmet of Shadows and became their commander.

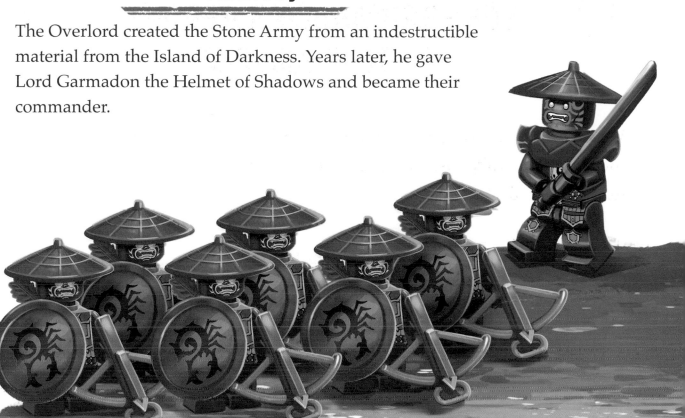

The Sons of Garmadon

Princess Harumi formed this biker gang with the goal of bringing Lord Garmadon back from the Departed Realm. After she succeeded, the Sons of Garmadon acted as Emperor Garmadon's police force in Ninjago City. Their motors were loud, but they had more flash than force.

TIME

"One master of Time was bad enough, but like the hands on a clock, there were two."
—Master Wu

Did Time begin before Creation, or did Time start when Creation began? Ninjago scholars have asked this question for years, but what we do know is that in the hands of the Masters of Time, the element of Time almost caused the destruction of Ninjago.

THE MASTERS OF TIME

Also known as the Time Twins, Krux and Acronix went to war with the other Elemental Masters over their belief that Time was the most powerful element.

Acronix

Krux

Acronix is a skilled combat fighter with a love for the modern technology that his brother despises. Acronix can:

- Slow down the field of time, causing a loss of speed.
- Move forward in time for a short period.

The (slightly) older Time Twin, Krux, disguised himself as Dr. Sanders Saunders for forty years, while his brother was trapped in a time vortex. Krux can:

- Pause time for a short period.
- Reverse time for a short period.

THE TIME BLADES

"The Hands of Time felt they controlled the most powerful element, therefore entitling them to rule all of Ninjago." —Master Wu

Years ago, the Elemental Masters formed the Elemental Alliance to battle the Serpentine—but Krux and Acronix sided with the snakes. Master of Fire, Ray, and Master of Water, Maya, forged four Time Blades. Each blade had the power to absorb one of the powers of the Time Twins. Wu and Garmadon used the Time Blades to strip Krux and Acronix of their powers and send them into a Temporal Vortex.

Krux escaped and plotted his revenge for years. He created an unbeatable metal tribe of Serpentine called the Vermillion. When Acronix escaped the Time Vortex, they recovered the Time Blades and created a machine that would guarantee the destruction of all the Elemental Masters: the Iron Doom.

THE IRON DOOM

This huge mech—a giant, human-controlled robot created by the Time Twins—could travel back and forth in time. Krux and Acronix brought the Vermillion Army back forty years, to the day they'd been defeated by the Elemental Alliance. They would have succeeded in destroying Ninjago if the ninja and Master Wu hadn't traveled back in time to stop them.

DID YOU KNOW?

Acronix delivered a Time Punch to Master Wu that aged him near death.

AMBER

"She is the Master of Amber, the power of absorption. She can emulate *the powers of anyone she's touched.*"
—Master Garmadon

The Master of Amber

A ninja with serious crossbow skills and an awesome power called Skylor was raised by her father, the evil Master Chen. Her friendship with Kai led her to turn against her father and help the ninja battle him.

Amber Power

Fire blasts! Water waves! Lightning strikes! Skylor can learn to perform any elemental attack once she has absorbed the power of another Elemental Master. She's more of a copycat than a thief—it seems the Master gets to keep their power, too.

Leading the Resistance

After the Tournament of Elements, Skylor took a break from fighting villains to run her father's noodle shop. But when the Sons of Garmadon seized control of Ninjago City, she emerged to lead the resistance, bringing several of the Elemental Masters back together.

The Staff of Elements

This ancient Anacondrai staff has a power that is eerily similar to Skylor's. It can be used to steal the powers of an Elemental Master, and anyone who wields the staff can use that power as their own. Master Chen created the Tournament of Elements as a plot to steal the powers of all the Elemental Masters—including those of his own daughter.

DID YOU KNOW?

Skylor's father, Master Chen, is not an Elemental Master. She got her powers from her mother, whose whereabouts are still unknown.

FORM

The Master of Form

Chamille, the Master of Form, faced off against Lloyd in a fierce round of Thunderblade roller derby in the Tournament of Elements. She lost to Lloyd but later joined the ninja to fight Master Chen. Today, all we know about her is that the Master of Metal says that she has become a "bad girl."

Greatest Moment

In the Thunderblade challenge, Jay gave Lloyd a boost by whipping him forward on the roller derby track. But it wasn't Lloyd who Jay helped—it was Chamille, tricking him!

Form Power

Purple-haired Chamille may stand out in a crowd, but she can get lost in one just as easily. She can change form to blend into the background, or shapeshift to look like anyone she wants to—even down to their voice and clothing. A true chameleon!

GRAVITY

"What goes up must always come down. Unless, of course, you are the Master of Gravity."
— Master Wu

The Master of Gravity

Gravis, the Master of Gravity, lost to Griffin Turner, the Master of Speed, in the Tournament of Elements. But he went on to become an important ally to the ninja team.

Gravity Power

Gravis can remove the field of gravity around him, which allows him to float or move at high speed. He can also levitate objects, or send them zooming through the air at his opponent.

Greatest Moment

When a huge stone statue toppled in the Corridor of Elders, Gravis used his powers to keep the statue from crushing his teammates.

LIGHT

The Master of Light

Mr. Pale sided with the ninja against Master Chen and the Anacondrai, and later joined the resistance against the Sons of Garmadon.

Light Power

The Master of Light manipulates light rays in order to appear invisible—allowing him to sneak into places undetected, or even sneak out of places he'd rather not be in. Cole found a way to counter Mr. Pale's invisibility—by coating him with rock dust to see his form.

Greatest Moment

When the Sons of Garmadon took over Ninjago City's airwaves, Mr. Pale helped take them back. He made sure Lloyd and the other members of the resistance slipped into Borg Tower without being seen.

METAL

"I get excited by metal."

—Karlof, the Master of Metal

The Master of Metal

Karlof lost to Kai in the Tournament of Elements, but he went on to befriend Cole when they were prisoners in Master Chen's Noodle Factory. Ever since then, he's become one of the ninjas' strongest allies.

Metal Power

Karlof's mighty metal fists can pound things into tiny bits. He can also turn his whole body into metal, making him an almost unbeatable opponent!

DID YOU KNOW?

Karlof worked as an aeronautical engineer in Metalonia, but he found he was happier just hammering opponents with his fists—like when he toppled supersized villain Killow with one punch!

MIND

The Master of Mind

Neuro was all set to compete against the ninja in the Tournament of Elements. But he sided with them after he read the mind of the sinister Clouse and learned of Master Chen's plot to reawaken the Anacondrai. He remains the ninja's friend.

Mind Power

As well as reading minds, Neuro can implant thoughts into minds. He can sense when someone is behind him and about to attack. And he can create mind waves that give his opponent a monster headache!

DID YOU KNOW?

It's not a good idea to play chess with Neuro. He can predict all your moves!

NATURE

The Master of Nature

Bolobo is a good-natured Elemental Master and friend to the ninja, but things haven't always gone his way. He lost to Neuro in the Tournament of Elements, and when the Sons of Garmadon took over Ninjago City, they put him in Kryptarium Prison.

DID YOU KNOW?

In the Tournament of Elements, Bolobo managed to pin the Lightning Ninja to the floor with his vines. Jay escaped by distracting Bolobo with a Fritz Donagan movie!

Nature Power

Bolobo can manipulate plants and natural environments. His signature move is to wrap his opponent in plant vines.

POISON

"More dangerous than the venom of a snake is the poison of anger when it overtakes your heart."
—Master Wu

The Master of Poison

With wild green hair and a wicked grin, Tox, the Master of Poison, looks like someone you don't want to mess with. The ninja were glad she decided to side with them against Master Chen and later, the Sons of Garmadon.

Poison Power

Tox blasts her opponents with a noxious cloud of toxic smoke. Scholars speculate that Tox may be immune to poison herself.

DID YOU KNOW?

Tox's poison blast didn't work against Master Chen's Anacondrai warriors. It's possible that their own venom neutralized the poison attack.

SHADOW

"That dude's throwing some serious shade!" —Griffin Turner, the Master of Speed

The Master of Shadow

It's hard to trust someone who lurks in the shadows, and the ninja thought Shade—the Master of Shadow—was a spy for Master Chen at first. But this shady Elemental Master was a loyal friend in the end.

Shadow Power

In combat, Shade can evade his opponent by disappearing into shadows and dark spaces.

DID YOU KNOW?

Shade can pass right through his opponent! He slipped through Master Garmadon to escape questioning by him and the ninja.

SMOKE

"I cause tears without sorrow." —Ninjigma riddle about Smoke

The Master of Smoke

In the Tournament of Elements, Ash, the Master of Smoke, tangled with two ninja: Lloyd and Kai. He battled with Lloyd over a Jade Blade, and he and Kai fought a fierce battle in the heart of a fiery volcano. His disappearing act kept both ninja on their toes.

Smoke Power

Smoke alarm! Ash can create a smoke screen to confuse his opponents. But even more impressive is his ability to become smoke to avoid attack.

DID YOU KNOW?

Ash went on to help the ninja defeat Master Chen, but no one has heard of him since.

SOUND

"Listen closely, and you can hear the heartbeat of the universe." —Master Wu

The Master of Sound

Jacob Pevsner, the Master of Sound, befriended the ninja during the tournament of elements. Today he lives a simple life surrounded by music, although his current whereabouts are unknown.

Sound Power

Jacob, who is blind, uses echolocation to shoot blow darts and throwing stars with perfect aim. This musical master uses a stringed instrument called a sitar to create powerful sound waves to attack his opponents.

Greatest Moment

When the last generation of Elemental Masters fought the Time Twins Krux and Acronix, the Master of Sound fought bravely, using his Sonic Scream against the Vermillion warriors.

SPEED

The Master of Speed

Turner wanted to beat the ninja in the Tournament of Elements but fast became an ally. He joined the resistance against the Sons of Garmadon.

Speed Power

Yes, he can move at superspeed, but that's not all. Turner's powers give him incredibly fast reflexes, the ability to jump really high, and impressive agility. The sheer force of his speed allows him to power up vertical obstacles, almost like he's defying gravity.

Greatest Moment

When the Sons of Garmadon attacked the ninja in an alley, Griffin arrived with some other Elemental Masters to save the day. Griffin speedily took down eight bikers in less than five seconds!

WIND

The Master of Wind

Most people get a chill when they hear the name Morro. This pupil of Master Wu's became obsessed with power after Wu told him he might be the Green Ninja. He ended up as a ghost in the Cursed Realm, who returned to Ninjago world to battle the ninja. These days, he resides peacefully in the Departed Realm.

Wind Power

The Master of Wind can control the wind, creating tornados and powerful gales to send opponents flying, or walls of air for defense. Ghostly Morro performed his wind attacks when he possessed the body of Lloyd.

Greatest Opponent

Morro's quest to become the Green Ninja led to an epic battle with Lloyd for the Realm Crystal that took place in midair, catapulted by Morro's winds. It ended with a victory for Morro—and Lloyd trapped in the Cursed Realm!

AMEET Sp. z o.o.
Nowe Sady 6, 94-102 Łódź—Poland
ameet@ameet.eu
www.ameet.eu
www.LEGO.com

Published in the United States by Random House Children's Books, a division of
Penguin Random House LLC, 1745 Broadway, New York, NY 10019, and in Canada by
Penguin Random House Canada Limited, Toronto. Random House and the colophon
are registered trademarks of Penguin Random House LLC.
rhcbooks.com
ISBN 978-0-593-38133-5 (trade) — ISBN 978-0-593-38135-9 (ebook)
Printed in the United States of America
10 9 8 7 6 5 4 3 2 1